Publisher: Thacher Books
ISBN 978-0-578-21183-1

Book Design: Joni Oeltjenbruns

It is with a grateful heart to God
that I dedicate this book to my grandson,
the real Boaz, and his parents.

Belly belly Boaz,
Belly belly Bo,
Itsy, bitsy you began,
Show us how you grow.

Belly belly Boaz,
Belly belly Bo,
Mama Boaz feeds you,
Bitsy belly grows.

Belly belly Boaz,
Belly belly Bo,
Daddy Boaz tickles,
Giggle belly Bo.

Belly belly Boaz,
Belly belly Bo,
Mama Boaz kisses,
Belly baby glows.

Belly belly Boaz, Belly belly Bo,

Roly-poly chubby, Over belly goes!

Belly belly Boaz,
Belly belly Bo,
Pokin' belly button,
Silly belly Bo.

A
B

Belly belly Boaz,
Belly belly Bo,
Fillin' jelly belly,
Whoa, baby, whoa!

Belly belly Boaz,
Belly belly Bo,
Bye-bye jelly belly,
Hello tippy-toe.

Belly belly Boaz,
Belly belly Bo,
Bobble wobble footsteps,
Ready, steady, go!

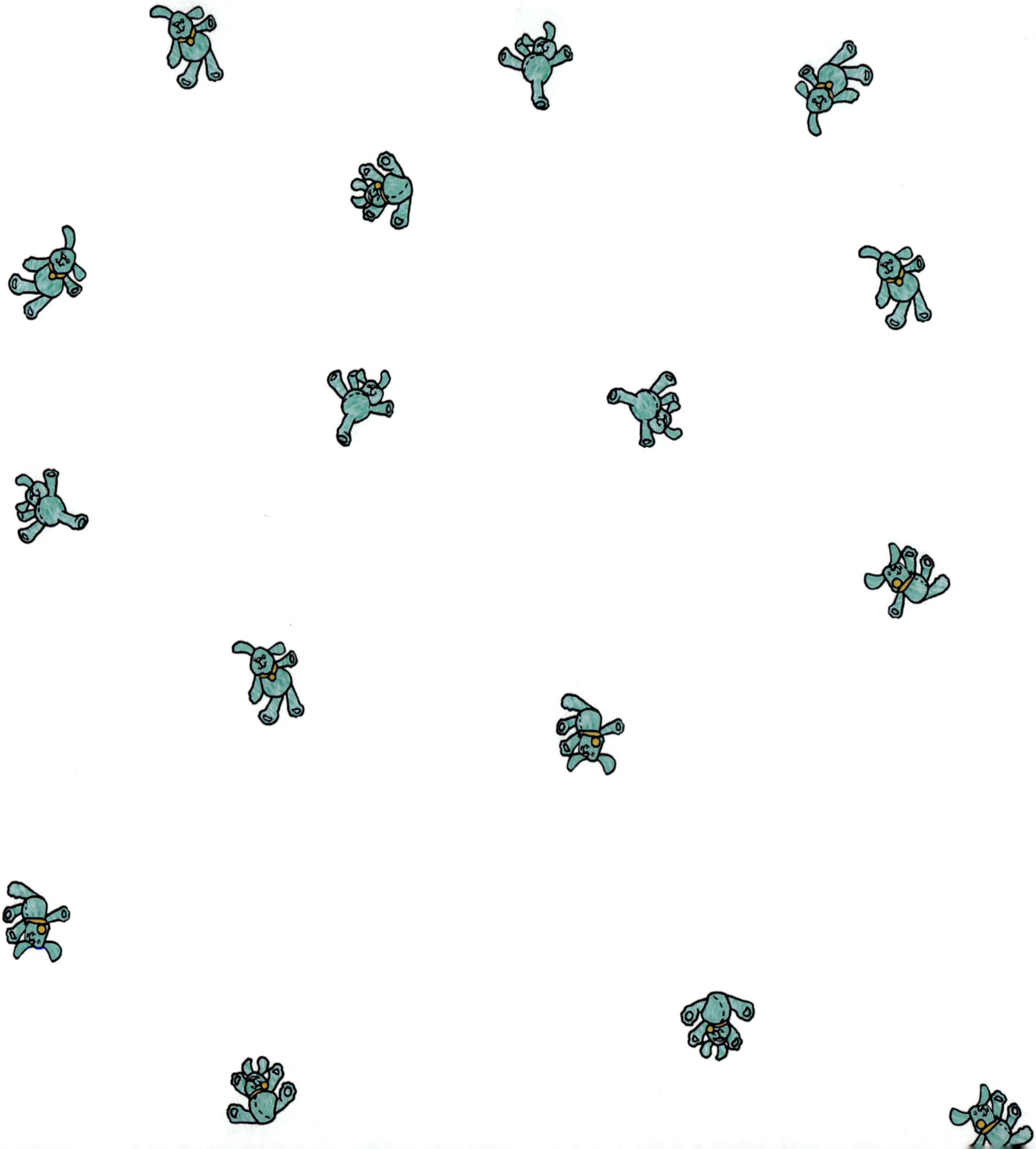

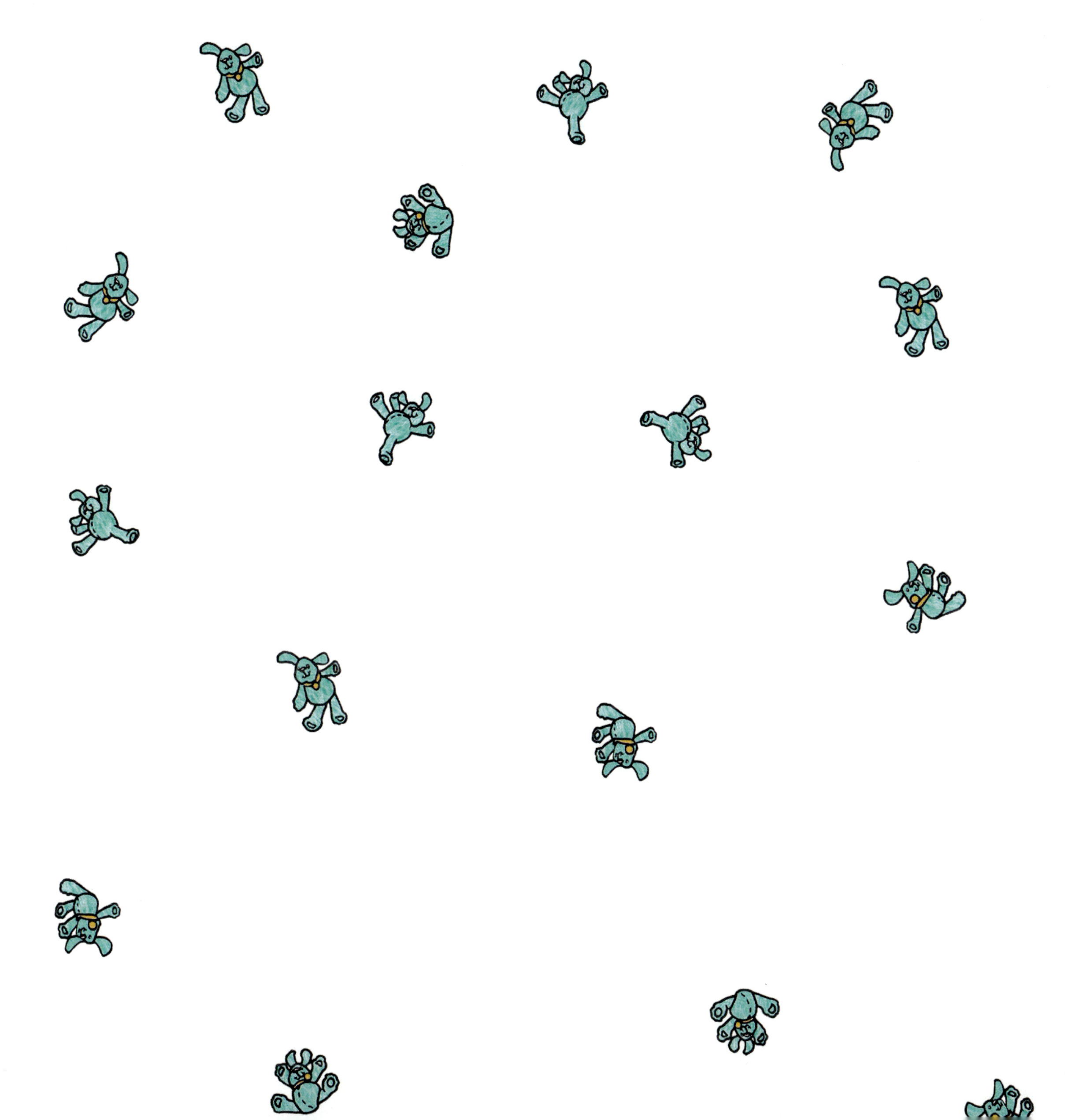

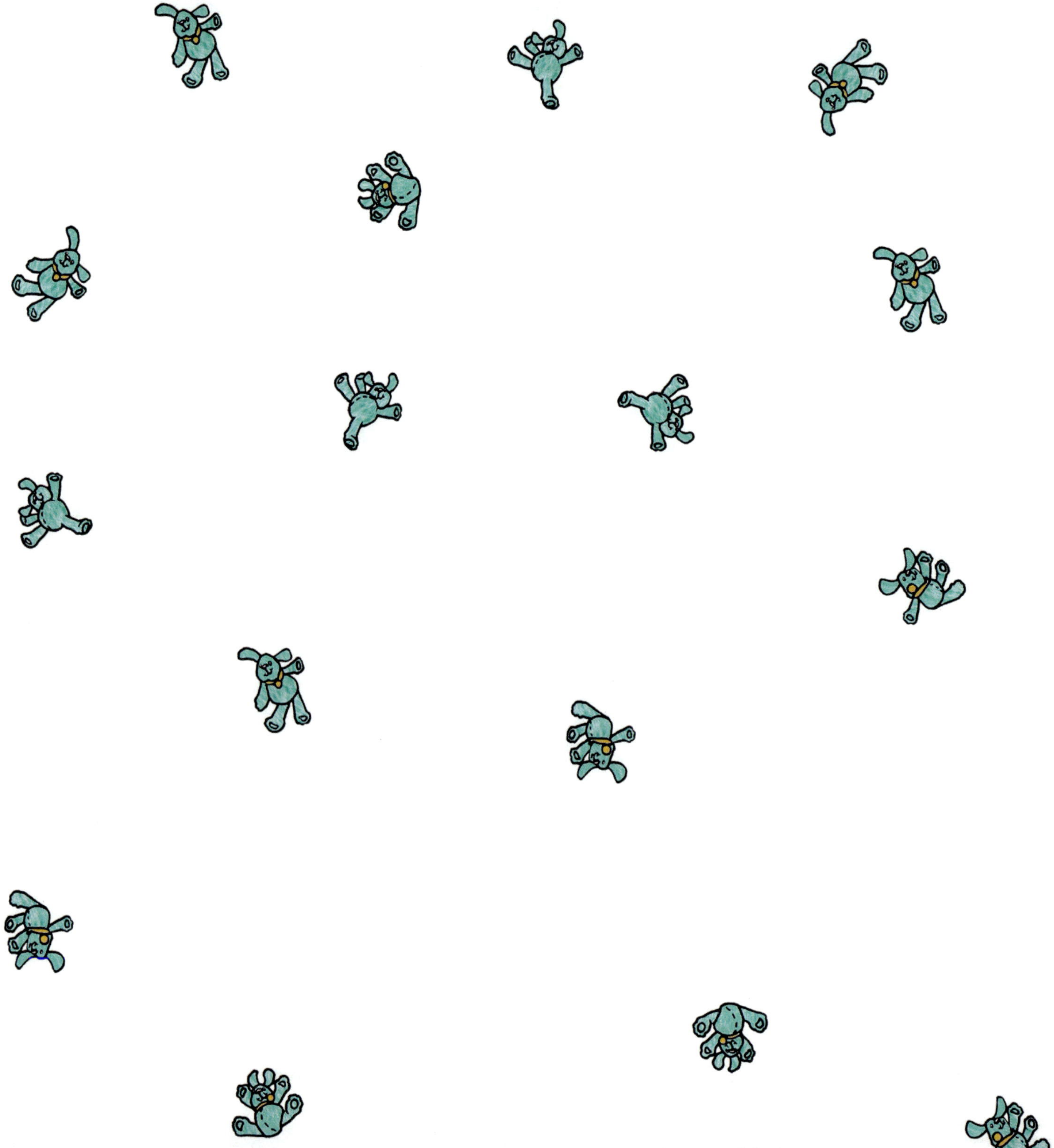